My Mom Is an OCTOPUS

Madaline McFarland

tate publishing
CHILDREN'S DIVISION

Published by Tate Publishing & Enterprises, LLC
127 E. Trade Center Terrace | Mustang, Oklahoma 73064 USA
1.888.361.9473 | www.tatepublishing.com

Tate Publishing is committed to excellence in the publishing industry. The company reflects the philosophy established by the founders, based on Psalm 68:11,
"The Lord gave the word and great was the company of those who published it."

Book design copyright © 2016 by Tate Publishing, LLC. All rights reserved.
Cover and interior design by Ralph Lim
Illustrations by Van Kevin Opura

Published in the United States of America

ISBN: 978-1-68254-021-3
1. Juvenile Fiction / Family / Parents
2. Juvenile Fiction / Social Issues / Values & Virtues
15.10.28

This book belongs to:

_____

It was Monday morning. I heard my mom say, "Time to get up!"

But I decided to sleep just a little bit longer.

"Hurry and get dressed," she said, but I was making a puppet show with my socks.

"Sweetie, you are running out of time. Go put on your shoes and get your backpack!"

But I was busy making faces with my cereal.

"Your little brother is already in the car. If you don't get moving now, you will be late for school."

So I hurried...a little.

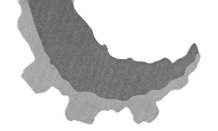

When we finally arrived at school, I was late! I couldn't believe it!

"Mom, why are we late again?" I asked.

"Well, honey, I am not a time machine. I tried to get you to hurry, but we just ran out of time."

While I was sitting at my desk, I started to think, *What if my mom was a time machine? I would never be late for school again. We could make all the time we wanted!*

Oh, and for vacation we could go back in time to visit dinosaurs!

But...what if Mom lost her keys and we got stuck?

I would have to sleep in a cave on a stone bed and learn how to invent TV! Maybe I don't want my mom to be a time machine.

Mom was on the phone when I climbed into the car. She gave me a wink and whispered, "Just a minute. Let me finish this call."

But I didn't want to wait. I had a very, *very* important question to ask about a snack and a slushy!

When she didn't answer, I decided to ask louder. Mom covered the phone and said, "Son, I want to hear everything you have to say just let me get off the phone. I don't have two heads, and I can only talk to one person at a time."

While I was waiting, I thought to myself, *What if my mom had two heads? Then she could talk on the phone and talk to me at the same time! Oh, and at bedtime she could read two books at once—one to me and one to my little brother.*

But...she might talk to herself too much, or even worse, when she went to kiss me good night, I'd get smooched from both sides. Maybe I don't want my mom to have two heads.

Home Sweet Home

While I was drinking my slushy in the backseat, my brother and I thought of a few questions.

"Mom, what is a brain freeze? How long would it take to drive to the moon? Do you know the difference between an alligator and a crocodile? How long would it take to count to one million and fifty-five?"

"One question at a time, guys," Mom said. "Besides, I don't think I know all of those answers. My head is not a computer, you know."

So I imagined...What if my mom's head was a computer? It would be great! I could ask her anything, and she would have the answer right away. Oh, and she would be great at playing computer games!

But...what if she was so good that she won every time and I always lost. What would happen if she got her head wet in the shower? She might short circuit and walk around all day saying, "Does not compute. Does not compute." Maybe I'm glad my mom's head is not a computer!

After school my brother and I were watching some TV. When our show ended, my brother yelled, "Mom! Mom! *Mommy!*"

Mom came running into the room to see what was wrong.

"Can you turn the channel?"

"What?" Mom said with a crazy look on her face. "I am not your maid. I love doing things for you and helping you, but sometimes you need to do things for yourselves."

Once Mom left the room, I thought how nice it would be if she was our maid. When we needed something, she would just be a bell ring away. That would be the life!

But then again, what if we asked her to do something special on the weekend and she said, "Sorry, I don't work on the weekends. By the way... you owe me one million and fifty-five dollars."

Okay, I guess I don't want my mom to be our maid.

While Mom was cooking dinner, I was creating a masterpiece from blocks. "Mom, look at this awesome plane I just built. You've got to see it."

"Oh, I know you are a great builder! I can't wait to see."

"Mom, it can't wait! You have to look now. Hurry before it's too late!"

"Honey, I am not an owl. I cannot turn my head all the way around. I will look when I finish cooking dinner. I know it is going to be a great surprise!"

Hmmm! An owl? What would happen if my mom was an owl? She would be great at flashlight tag. Oh, and we would have the coolest tree house in the neighborhood! But then...what if she served dead mice for dinner, or even worse, what if she tried to feed me like an owlet? *Gross!* I am glad my mother is not an owl.

When Mom was doing dishes, I asked if we could play a game. My brother asked if she could mend a hole in his teddy. "Honey," Dad said, "have you seen the remote?"

"Hold on, everyone," Mom said. "I am not an octopus! I love helping all of you, but I only have two hands and can only do one thing at a time."

Wait a minute! An octopus? What would happen if my mom was an octopus? We would have a great time in the pool. If I dropped something in the deep end, she could get it. Easy peasy!

But...what would bedtime be like? She might brush my teeth, comb my hair, and clean out my ears all at the same time and still have hands left over! Even though she could do lots of things at once, I'm glad my mom is not an octopus.

As I was waiting for her to come and play our game, I looked down at my own arms. Hmmm, I have two arms and so does my brother. My dad has two arms and so does my mother.

My mom doesn't have eight arms, but if we used all of our arms, we could be an octopus together.

Thanks for joining us on our daily adventure. Now that I have put some big questions in little heads, I thought it was only fair to answer them.

What is a brain freeze?

Do you mean what is a sphenopalatine ganglioneuralgia?

Well, that is the real name for it. A brain freeze is caused from eating or drinking something really cold really fast. When the temperature changes quickly in the back of your throat, it causes the arteries that go to the brain to contract. The brain is sent an alert message that something changed too fast and that causes your freeze or headache.

Good news though! A brain freeze can go away as fast as it came. Just drink some warm water or hold your warm tongue to the roof of your mouth. As the temperature returns to normal, your brain freeze will melt away.

Source: Wake Forest Baptist Medical Center. *Neuroscientists Explain How the Sensation of Brain Freeze Works.* May 22, 2013. *http://www.sciencedaily. com/releases/2013/05/130522095335.htm*

How long would it take to drive to the moon?

The moon is about 239,000 miles away from the earth. If a person could drive to the moon and traveled at a speed of 65 miles per hour, it would take them approximately 3,677 hours or 153 days. That is, of course, if you don't make any pit stops for a Milky Way shake and other space snacks. How did I figure that out? It's just math!

239,000 miles / 65 miles per hour = 3,677 hours

3,677 hours / 24 hours in a day =153 days

You can find out more cool stuff about the moon here: http://www.planetsforkids.org/moon-moon.html

What are the differences between an alligator and a crocodile?

I guess you could call these guys creature cousins because they come from the same animal family called Crocodylia. Crocodiles are much more aggressive, often live in salt water, and can be found all over the world. Alligators are usually smaller. They live in fresh water and are only found in the United States and China. Crocodiles have a larger V-shaped head while alligators have a smaller U-shaped head. However, if you don't want to get too close to investigate, there is one way to tell the difference from farther away. Crocodiles like to show their teeth. The fourth one on either side to be exact, it sticks out when his mouth is closed. I think he might be showing off a little bit or trying to trick us with a crooked smile.

Source: Science Kids. *Animal Facts. Crocodile & Alligator Differences.* N.p. July 2014. http:// www.sciencekids.co.nz/sciencefacts/animals/ crocodilealligatordifferences.html

How long would it take to count to one million and fifty-five?
Well, that is a pretty big number! Let's start with what we do know.
1 day = 24 hours
1 hour = 60 minutes
24 x 60 = 1,440 minutes per day
1 minute = 60 seconds in a day
1,440 x 60 = 86,400 seconds

1,000,055 / 86,400 = 11.57 days

So if you did nothing else but count, no eating, sleeping, or bathroom breaks, it would take you eleven and one half days to count to one million and fifty-five.

Wow! I guess a million really is a big number!

Remember, this math works only if you are counting one number per second.

Never forget! It is always good to ask questions. Just make sure you try to stay patient until you can look up the answer. Oh, and never get on the Internet without your parent's permission.

Stay safe and remember to help your mom out every now and then!

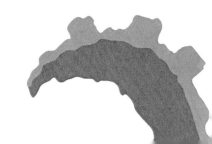

e|LIVE

listen|imagine|view|experience

AUDIO BOOK DOWNLOAD INCLUDED WITH THIS BOOK!

In your hands you hold a complete digital entertainment package. In addition to the paper version, you receive a free download of the audio version of this book. Simply use the code listed below when visiting our website. Once downloaded to your computer, you can listen to the book through your computer's speakers, burn it to an audio CD or save the file to your portable music device (such as Apple's popular iPod) and listen on the go!

How to get your free audio book digital download:

1. Visit www.tatepublishing.com and click on the e|LIVE logo on the home page.
2. Enter the following coupon code:
   f957-f207-39c0-0e95-1965-1e71-0267-33ce
3. Download the audio book from your e|LIVE digital locker and begin enjoying your new digital entertainment package today!

31869104R00018

Made in the USA
San Bernardino, CA
21 March 2016